W9-BSL-829

For Louisa —BB

For Worth, Adlai, and Alouette —EB

About This Book: The illustrations for this book were done in pencil and watercolor. This book was edited by Andrea Spooner and designed by Nicole Brown with art direction by David Caplan. The production was supervised by Erika Schwartz, and the production editor was Jen Graham. The text was set in Perpetua.

Text copyright © 2019 by Ben Brashares • Illustrations copyright © 2019 by Elizabeth Bergeland • Cover illustration copyright © 2019 by Elizabeth Bergeland. • Cover design by Nicole Brown • Cover copyright © 2019 by Hachette Book Group, Inc. • Hachette Book Group supports the right to free expression and the value of copyright. The purpose of copyright is to encourage writers and artists to produce the creative works that enrich our culture. • The scanning, uploading, and distribution of this book without permission is a theft of the author's intellectual property. If you would like permission to use material from the book (other than for review purposes), please contact permissions@hbgusa.com. Thank you for your support of the author's rights. • Little, Brown and Company • Hachette Book Group • 1290 Avenue of the Americas, New York, NY 10104 • Visit us at LBYR.com • First Edition: May 2019 • Little, Brown and Company is a division of Hachette Book Group, Inc. The Little, Brown name and logo are trademarks of Hachette Book Group, Inc. • The publisher is not responsible for websites (or their content) that are not owned by the publisher. • Library of Congress Cataloging-in-Publication Data • Names: Brashares, Ben, author. | Bergeland, Elizabeth, illustrator. • Title: Being Edie is hard today / written by Ben Brashares ; illustrated by Elizabeth Bergeland. • Description: First edition. | New York ; Boston : Little, Brown and Company, 2019. | Summary: A sensitive girl imagines transforming herself into different animals to help manage her intense emotions during difficult situations at school. • Identifiers: LCCN 2018020158 | ISBN 9780316521741 (hardcover) | ISBN 9780316521710 (ebook) | ISBN 9780316521758 (library edition ebook) • Subjects: | CYAC: Emotions—Fiction. | Behavior—Fiction. | Animals—Fiction. | Schools—Fiction. • Classification: LCC PZ7.1.B751536 Be 2019 | DDC [E]—dc23 • LC record available at https://lccn.loc.gov/2018020158 • ISBNs: 978-0-316-52174-1 (hardcover), 978-0-316-52172-7 (ebook), 978-0-316-52171-0 (ebook), 978-0-316-52173-4 (ebook) • PRINTED IN CHINA • APS • 10 9 8 7 6 5 4 3 2 1

Being Edie

Is Hard Today

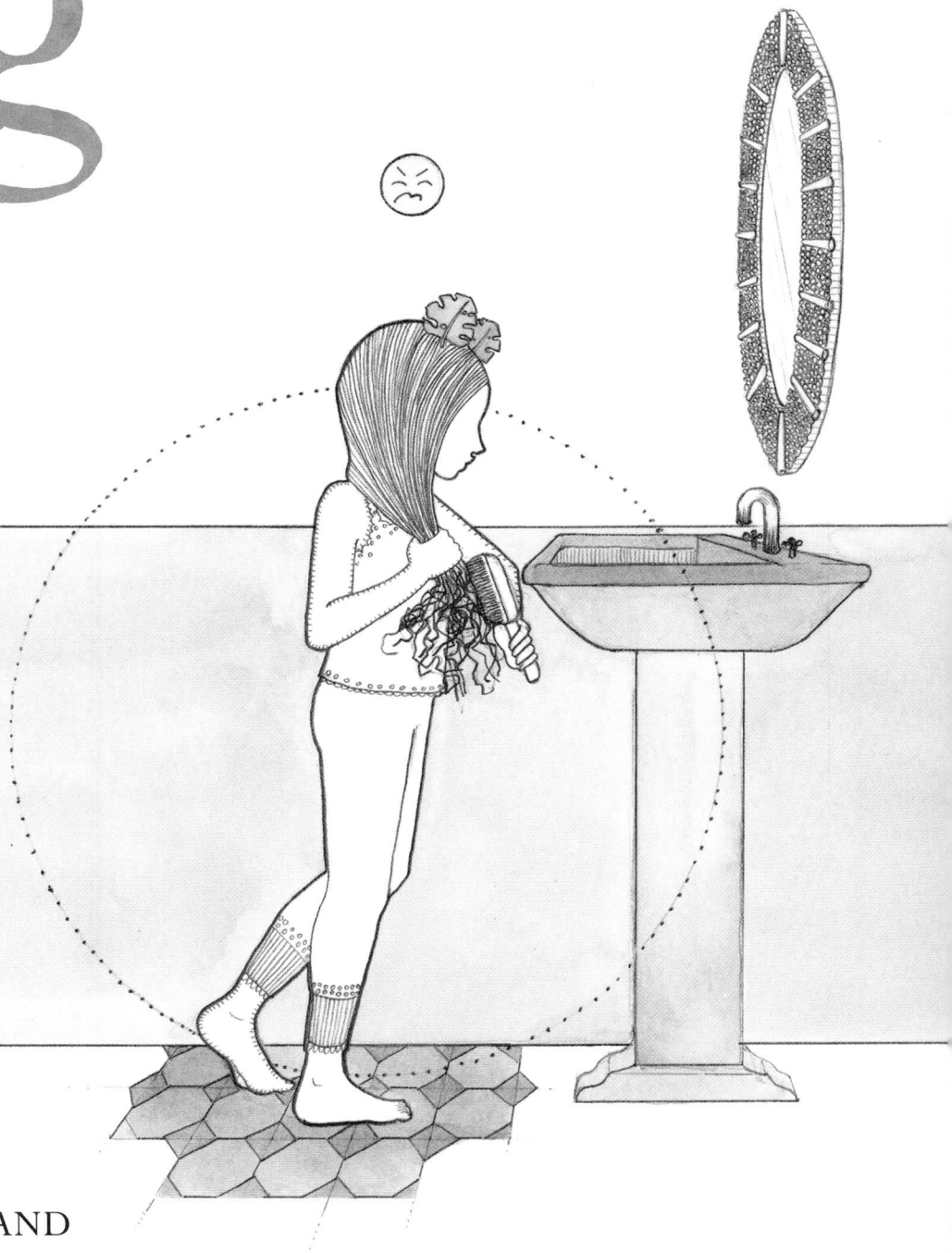

Written by BEN BRASHARES
Illustrated by ELIZABETH BERGELAND

Little, Brown and Company
New York Boston

Being Edie was hard today.
She barely made it to breakfast.
"Please eat your toast, Edie," her mom said.
"I'm too tired to eat my toast," Edie replied.
"Please sit up, Edie," her mom said.
"I can't," Edie said. "My head is too heavy."

"Pony or piggy?" her mom asked while
they waited for the school bus.
"Piggy, please, Mother," Edie answered.
When the bus arrived, Edie reminded her
mother that piggies don't go to school.
"This little piggy does," her mom said,
and scooted Edie out the door.

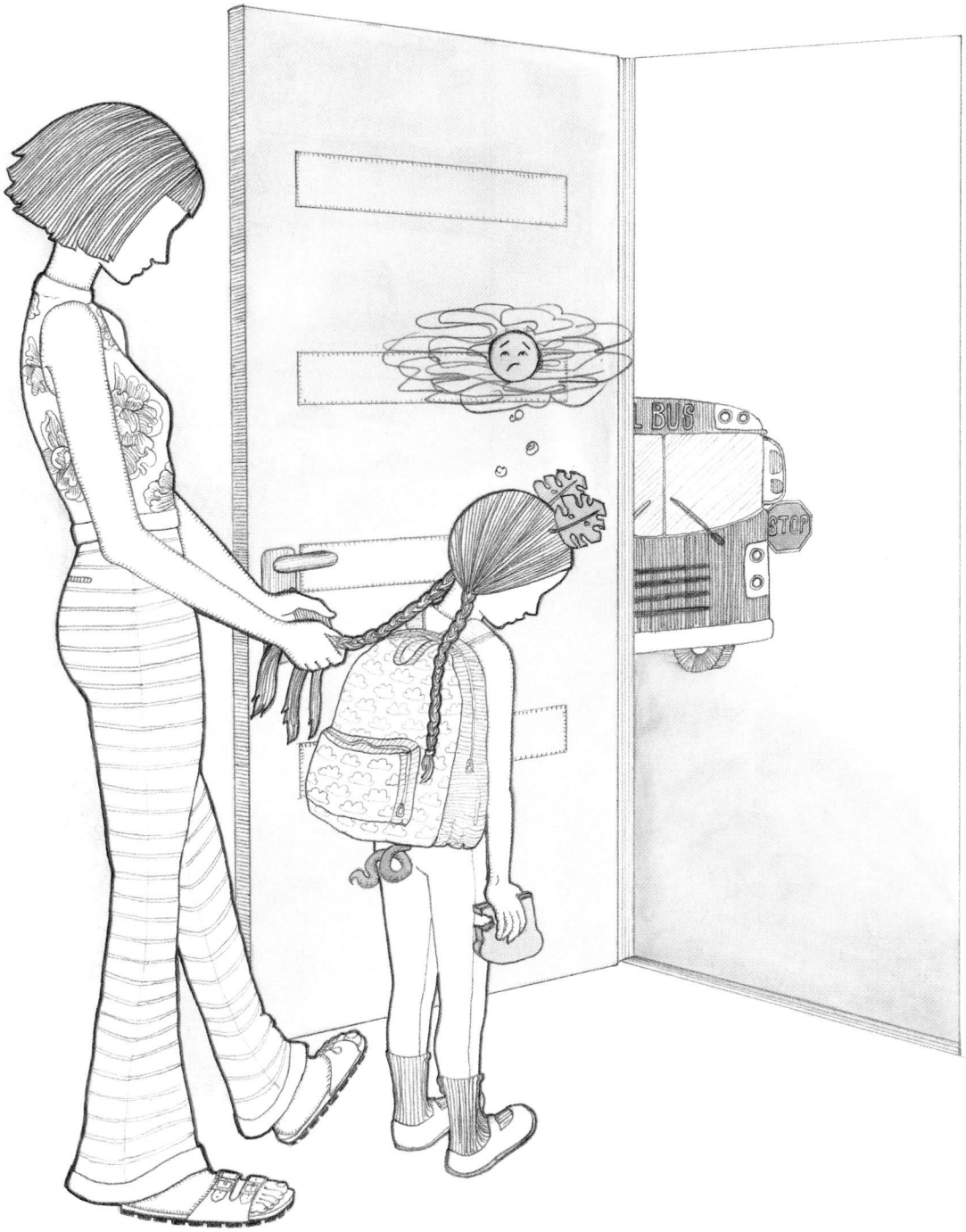
BUS
STOP

She had made a mistake. A pony would have been much better.

While putting her things away,
Edie thought for a moment about
climbing into her cubby.
Maybe just hanging there.
Like a bat.
Until it was time to go home.

Edie

In class, Ms. Meany called on Edie to write on the board, but Edie didn't know the answer.

"I can't," she said.
"Why can't you, Edie?"
"I have polar bear hands,"
she said, and showed her.

At recess, Edie sat in her favorite spot and ate her favorite snack (sardines).
"Only squids eat sardines," one boy said.
"Edie, the stinky squid!" they sang. "EE-dee-the-STINK—ee-SQUID!"
And they circled her like sharks.

Oh, to be a squid.

P.U.

Alone, she sat on the swing where she'd go to think
and imagine she had great wings that could take her high above.
But the wings never worked.

So she decided to be a cheetah,
the fastest, fiercest land animal on earth.

Her stomach grumbled.
The lunch bell rang.

And she was off.

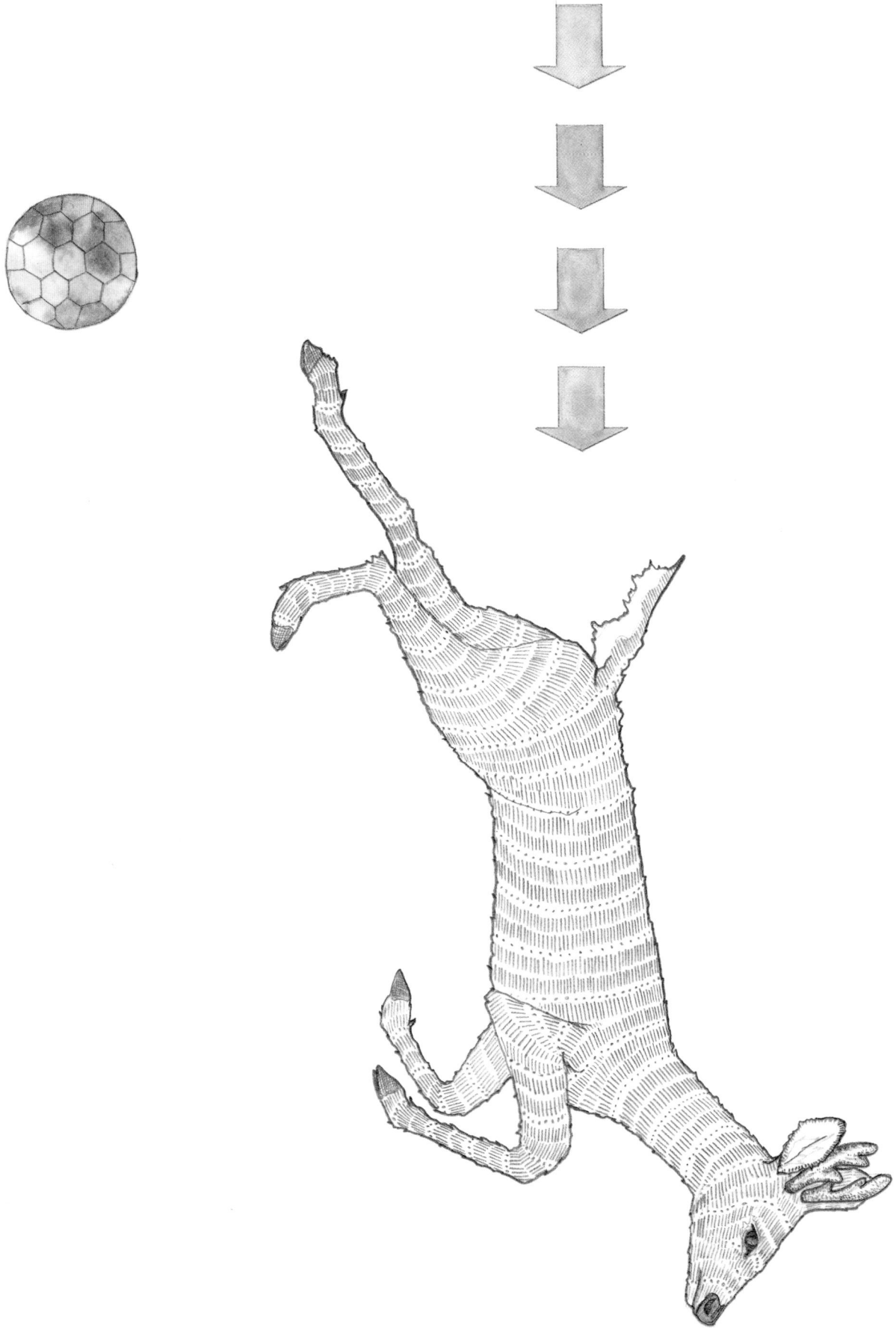

During her rather long trip to the principal's office, Edie tried to explain the slow-moving characteristics of a sloth, but Ms. Meany wasn't listening.

Edie figured if she just. Sat. Still enough....
the principal probably wouldn't see her.

"Edie. Edie. Edie? Eeeeeeeeedeeeeeeee!"

Chameleon was definitely the right choice.

For the ride home,
Edie considered a porcupine
or a hissing cockroach.
Eventually she decided to be an armadillo.

But inside, she felt like a naked mole rat.

At dinner, Edie was lost in thought.

"Edie, would you like to use your fork?" her mom asked.

"No, thank you, Mother. This is how butterflies taste their food."

When it was time for bed, Edie found that she had, unfortunately, become a worm.
"EDIE! 'EASE come 'rush your teesh!"

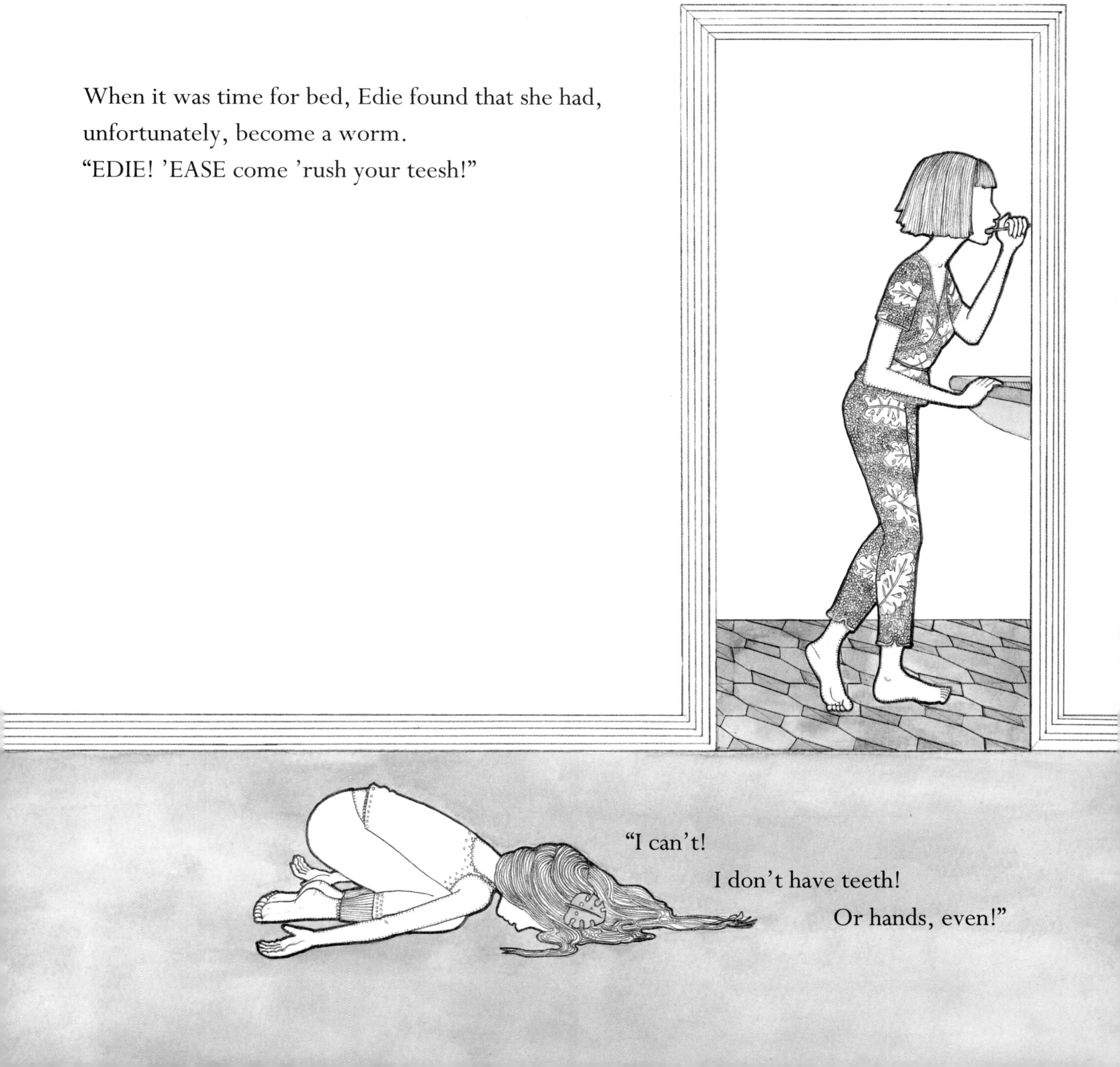

"I can't!
I don't have teeth!
Or hands, even!"

"Honey, come pick out your clothes for school tomorrow,"
Edie's mom called from the other room.
"Worms don't go to school!" Edie yelled back.

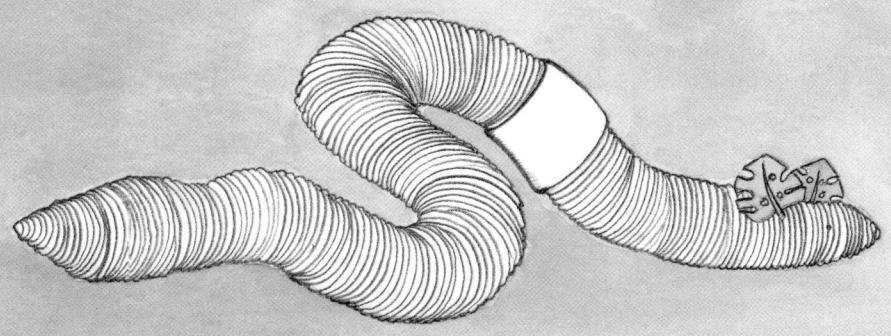

But her mom didn't hear her.
Because people can't hear worms.

The floor was uncomfortable, so Edie found her feet and pulled herself up to the mirror. She hoped to see something new.

But she only saw Edie.
Edie, who had to go to school tomorrow.

Edie sat on her bed and held her knees as tears filled her eyes.
"Mom?" she said. "I don't think I want to go to school tomorrow."
Just saying the words made the tears jump out.
Her mom stroked her arm and let her cry.

"Did you know," her mom finally said, reaching out to collect a tear, "that humans are the only creatures on earth that cry tears when they're sad? And no one really knows why."
Edie looked up and wiped her eyes. "I think *I* do. It's just like why the sky cries when it's sad," she said.

"I learned about it in school," Edie went on. "The clouds get dark and fill up with tears and then, when the clouds can't hold any more, the tears fall all the way down to the ground, where they help make flowers grow and make streams for animals to drink out of and take baths in...."

Edie's mom smiled. "So...does the sky feel better after it cries?"

"Oh yeah," Edie said. "The clouds get all fluffy again, and the sun comes out."
"You feeling a little fluffier?" her mom asked, pulling her in for a hug.
"Yeah. I guess. Like a fluffy baby owl. Owls are nocturnal, you know,
so I'm going to stay up all—"
"Night night, Edie."

"Pony or piggy?" her mom asked the next morning.
"Piggy, please, Mother," Edie replied. "No, wait—pony!"
"You sure?" her mom asked.
"Pony *and* piggy...and anteater, frog, lemur, lion, hedgehog, and...flying squirrel."
"Okay, but no cheetahs today." Her mom kissed the top of her head. "Better yet, how about you just go as my favorite little girl Edie?"
Edie thought for a moment.

"Yeah, okay. I guess being Edie's pretty good, too."